There once was a shepherd boy.

The only thing he ever saw was sheep.

One day, the shepherd had an idea.

The townsfolk ran to help him.

But there was no wolf.

10

The next day, the boy became bored again.

'He would not try to trick us twice'
the townsfolk said.

'You are so foolish to be tricked again!' the boy said.

16

'You should not tell lies!' yelled the townsfolk.

The next day, a wolf sprang out of the woods.

20

The townsfolk thought he was trying to trick them again.

23

The boy wondered why nobody came to help.

Finally, the flock reached town.

The moral of the story is:

Nobody believes a liar, even when he tells the truth.

SHORT TALES
Fairy Tales

Titles in the Short Tales Fairy Tales series:

Aladdin and the Lamp

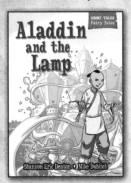

978 0 7502 7750 1

Beauty and the Beast

978 0 7502 7752 5

Jack and the Beanstalk

978 0 7502 7751 8

Puss in Boots

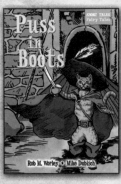

978 0 7502 7754 9

Sleeping Beauty

978 0 7502 7755 6

The Little Mermaid

978 0 7502 7753 2

WAYLAND
www.waylandbooks.co.uk

Follow us on Twitter @waylandbooks | Find us on Facebook Wayland Books

SHORT TALES
Fables

Titles in the Short Tales Fables series:

The Ants and the Grasshopper

978 0 7502 7756 3

The Boy who cried Wolf

978 0 7502 7757 0

The Fox and the Grapes

978 0 7502 7758 7

The Lion and the Mouse

978 0 7502 7783 9

The Tortoise and the Hare

978 0 7502 7784 6

The Town Mouse and the Country Mouse

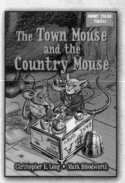

978 0 7502 7785 3

WAYLAND
www.waylandbooks.co.uk

Follow us on Twitter @waylandbooks | Find us on Facebook Wayland Books